Disappearing Granny

Sheila Lavelle

Illustrated by
LISA KOPPER

HEINEMANN·LONDON

To Barrie Roberts, the ideas man

William Heinemann Ltd
10 Upper Grosvenor Street, London W1X 9PA

LONDON · MELBOURNE · TORONTO
JOHANNESBURG · AUCKLAND

First published 1985

A school pack of BANANA BOOKS 7–12 is
available from Heinemann Educational Books
ISBN 0 435 00101 9

434 93026 1
Printed in Hong Kong by
Imago Publishing Ltd

Chapter One

WHEN BEN CAME home from school that chilly Friday afternoon in November, he had no idea of the horrible things that were going to happen to him that evening. He whistled a tune from Top of the Pops and thought only of fish and chips for tea and what might be on the telly.

Ben's sister Polly was sitting on the back doorstep of the cottage. She shuffled sideways to let Ben past.

'All right, Polly?' said Ben. 'Where's Mam?'

'Having a rest,' said Polly, grinning up at her brother. 'We been baking apple pies.'

Ben went into the kitchen and hung his satchel on the back of the door. The house smelt warm and spicy and three pies stood cooling on a tray. His mother was sitting on the floor, staring at the wall. Her back was straight and a pile of books was balanced on her head.

'Your money or your life,' Ben hissed into his mother's ear, jabbing a finger into her ribs. She gave a loud shriek and the books crashed to the floor.

'Ben,' she said crossly, getting up and pushing her hair out of her eyes. 'That wasn't funny.'

'I think it was,' said Ben. He shook the biscuit tin to see if it rattled, and when it didn't he put it down again

with a sigh. 'Can I have a bit of pie?' he said hopefully.

'Not now, Ben,' said his mother. 'You'll spoil your tea.' She put the books away on a shelf and began to wrap one of the pies in a clean tea-towel. 'I want you to run down to Granny Price's with this,' she said.

Ben started backing towards the door.

'Not me, Mam,' he said. 'I'm not

going down that spooky place. Granny Price is a witch.'

'Don't be silly, Ben,' said his mother. 'She's just a hard-up old woman, too proud to live on social security.'

'Granny Price is a witch,' repeated Ben. 'Everybody says so. She eats bats and toads and stuff. She keeps big black spiders in cages. I'm not going down there.'

Ben's mother finished wrapping the pie and pushed it into his hands.

'Granny Price collects mushrooms in the woods, that's all. If she didn't, she'd probably starve. So you can just do as you're told, bonny lad.'

She pushed Ben out of the door. 'It'll only take you half an hour. And you can take Polly with you. Give me a bit of peace for a change.' And she shut the door in his face.

Ben swore under his breath.

'Ee, Ben,' said Polly, widening her eyes. 'I'll tell Mam you said that word.'

Ben leaned down and put his face close to hers.

'You better not,' he whispered. 'Or I'll bite your tongue out and give it to that scabby ginger cat next door.'

Polly began to wail loudly and Ben glanced fearfully towards the kitchen door.

'Shurrup, Polly,' he said hastily. 'I didn't mean it. Come on, you can have a nice ride on the cart.'

Polly's tears disappeared like magic,

and she trotted eagerly down the back garden with Ben to the shed.

Ben opened the shed door and dragged out the wooden cart by its string. He had made the whole thing himself, and it was the biggest and most beautiful cart in the world. Built from two old pram chassis, it had eight wheels and was six feet long. Wooden planks formed the base, a good strong crate made a seat, and there was even a steering wheel that Mr Hamburger, the scrap dealer, had given him. All the cart needed now was a coat of paint, and

Ben had been saving his pocket money for weeks to pay for it.

Giving Polly the pie to hold, Ben lifted her into the seat. He fastened the toggles on her duffle coat and tucked her hair under the hood. Then he pulled his woolly hat well down over his ears and set off down the lane towards the village, towing the cart behind him.

Chapter Two

THE CART ROLLED through the village square and along the High Street, passing the lighted windows of the paper shop just as a familiar figure was coming out. Danny Brannigan, the son of a county rugby player, was tall and broad like his father. He was also Ben's best friend, and Ben had never been so pleased to see him in his life.

'Come with us, Danny?' he said. 'We're going down Whistling Woods.'

'All right,' said Danny, falling into step beside Ben. He tore open a packet of cheese and onion crisps and offered them first to Ben and then to Polly.

'It's not half cold,' he said, pulling the collar of his anorak up around his ears. 'What you going down Whistling Woods for on a day like this?'

'My mam sent me,' said Ben gloomily. 'I've got to take a pie to that weird old woman.'

Danny stopped on the pavement and stared at Ben. 'Not Granny Price,' he said, round-eyed. 'We'll get turned into frogs or something.'

'Aw, don't talk daft, Danny,' said Ben. 'None of that stuff's true.'

'It better not be,' said Danny, thrusting his hands deep into his pockets and starting off across the common. And Ben couldn't help giving a shiver as he hurried after his friend.

The old house on the edge of the Whistling Woods looked as if nobody had lived there for years. The paintwork was so cracked and peeling that it was hard to tell what colour it had once been. Ben stopped the cart outside the gate and took the pie from Polly.

'You've been eating it,' he said, looking down at the hole in the crust.

'Only a tiny bit,' said Polly. 'I was hungry.'

Ben scowled at his sister in disgust. Then he quickly re-wrapped the pie in the cloth and pushed open the broken wooden gate. The house looked so dark and scary that Ben's stomach squirmed like a bucket of worms. He knew he couldn't go in on his own.

'Come on, Danny,' he said. 'Polly

can mind the cart. We'll only be a minute.'

The two boys made their way up the path to the front porch. A faint light flickered through the window of the front room as Ben groped for the doorknocker and gave it three good raps.

'There's nobody in,' said Danny after a minute. 'She's gone for a ride on her broomstick.'

'Shurrup, will you,' said Ben with a shudder. 'Maybe she just didn't hear.' He banged louder and kicked at the peeling paint. 'She must be as deaf as a dustbin.'

'Leave the pie on the step,' suggested Danny.'It's all you can do.'

'She might not find it,' said Ben. 'A dog or something might get it.' He shook his head unhappily. 'No, I reckon we should go in. My mam will only send me back if we don't.'

Ben lifted the latch and the door creaked open. The boys saw a dark passage and another door in front of them. Firelight flickered in the room beyond.

'Granny Price?' called Ben, and his voice came out in a strange sort of squeak. 'Granny Price? It's me, Ben Gibson.'

The boys listened intently, but all they could hear was their own breathing. After a moment Ben pushed open the second door. The two friends stood together on the threshold, gazing fearfully into the silent room.

The fire had burnt low so that only a flicker lit the shadows. In front of the fireplace Ben could just make out the shape of a rocking chair. And slumped sideways in the chair, her head lolling on her neck, was Granny Price.

A prickle went up Ben's spine and his feet felt like concrete.

'Is she asleep?' whispered Danny hoarsely. 'Give her a nudge.'

Ben forced himself to take a couple of steps forward. As he drew nearer he saw that the old woman had a bowl of

half-eaten food in her lap. Something black and slimy. Something that made Ben's stomach heave so that he was almost sick on the carpet.

'Yuck,' he breathed in disgust. 'Toadstools.'

The old woman's eyes were closed and Ben leaned over and shook her gently by the shoulder.

'Gug . . . gug . . . Granny Price?' he croaked. 'Are you all right?'

Ben leapt back in horror and his hair stood on end as Granny Price slowly slithered forward and toppled to the floor with a thud.

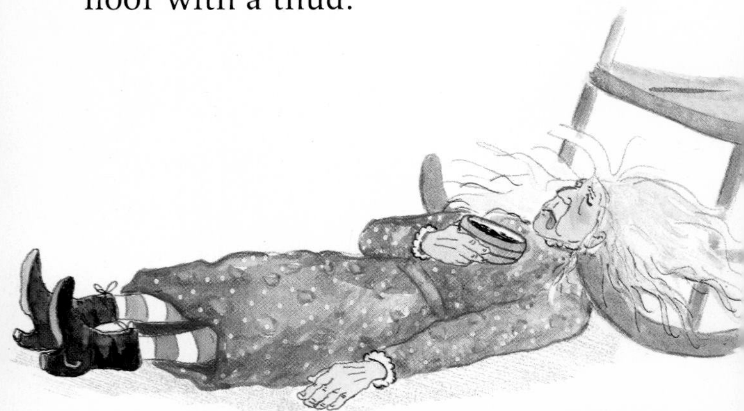

Chapter Three

BEN AND DANNY stood trembling together in the porchway and stared at one another with bulging eyes.

'You don't think she's . . . gone, do you?' said Danny weakly. 'She's not . . . er . . . you know?' His face looked as pale as a rice pudding in the darkness.

'Must have been them toadstools,' said Ben, trying to sound brave. 'I bet they were poisonous.'

'What are we gonna do?' said Danny, shivering from cold and fright.

Ben tried to decide what was the best thing to do. They had to get help, call a doctor or something. But somehow he didn't like the idea of leaving that poor old woman lying there, all on her own like that. It didn't seem right.

'Listen, Danny,' he said. 'I better run across the common and get Doctor Brown. You stay here and keep an eye on things. I'll not be long.' He started off down the path, but Danny grabbed at his arm in panic.

'No fear, mate,' he said. 'I'm not stopping here on my own with that . . . that . . .'

'You've got to, Danny,' Ben interrupted. 'We can't just go off and leave her, can we? Someone always has to stay with the . . . the . . . person. One of us will have to stay.'

'You stay then,' said Danny promptly. 'I'll get the doctor. I can run faster than you anyway.' And he headed towards the gate.

Ben thought of what lay inside on the floor and his heart sank into his wellies.

'Wait,' he said quickly. 'I've got a better idea. We'll take her with us. On the cart.' It seemed such a sensible solution he wondered why he hadn't thought of it before.

Danny turned round slowly and his pale face turned even whiter.

'You're not right in the head, Ben Gibson,' he said. 'I'm having nothing more to do with it. I'm going home.'

There came a sudden loud wailing from out in the lane. Polly, growing colder and more fed-up by the minute, had started to howl. Ben made one last appeal to his friend's loyalty.

'Come on, Dan,' he said. 'Are you gonna help me or not? I can't do anything on my own.'

Danny hunched his shoulders and stared at the ground.

'All right,' he muttered at last. 'Let's get it over with.'

Calling to Polly that they'd be coming soon, the two boys hurried back into the house. The old woman still lay where they had left her on the floor. Ben had trouble stopping his teeth from chattering.

'Wrap her up in the carpet,' he whispered to Danny. 'We don't want our Polly screaming the place down.'

Danny pushed the heavy rocking-chair off to one side while Ben, trying not to look at her face, straightened Granny Price's limp body out on the floor. Then together they rolled her up

in the threadbare carpet and dragged the bundle out through the front door and down the path to the gate.

Polly stopped wailing and stared.

'What's that?' she sniffed, wiping her nose on the sleeve of her duffle coat.

'Get off the cart, Polly, will you?' said Ben. 'We've got to take this old carpet round to Doctor Brown's.' He prayed his sister wouldn't make a fuss.

'*He* won't want it,' said Polly, peering at the long sausage shape in the darkness. But she climbed down willingly enough, and Ben breathed a sigh of relief.

Getting Granny Price onto the cart in Polly's place was not so easy, however, and Ben was grateful for the strong shoulders of his friend. Together they managed it at last, and set off on the long haul back across the common towards the village.

Chapter Four

POLLY SOON TIRED of trudging along behind.

'Why can't I sit on top?' she complained after a while, and Ben's heart missed a beat at the very thought.

'You might as well let her,' said Danny reasonably. 'It's not going to make a lot of difference now, is it?

So Polly was lifted up to sit astride the rolled-up carpet, where she amused herself by clicking her tongue and

shouting, 'Gee-up, horsie,' as if she were riding a donkey on Tynemouth beach. If she only knew what it was she was sitting on, Ben thought with a hysterical giggle.

The cart rolled into the village at last, and the lighted streets and the shops made Ben feel better at once. In just a few more minutes this horrible nightmare would be over, and he could pretend that none of it had ever happened.

Ben stopped the cart outside the doctor's surgery and turned to his friend.

'I'll go in and get Doctor Brown,' he said. 'You stay out here with Polly. Right?'

'All right,' said Danny glumly. 'Then can I go home for me tea?'

'Just as soon as we get the doctor,'

promised Ben, pushing open the door of the waiting-room.

About a dozen patients waited on benches round the room. They read magazines, chatted, coughed and sneezed and blew their noses, and they all stared at Ben as he tapped at the sliding window of the receptionist's office.

Ben cleared his throat as the window slid promptly open and Mrs Allen glared out at him. Mrs Allen had a sour face and a turned-down mouth as if she sucked lemons for a hobby.

'I have to see the doctor,' said Ben in a small voice.

'Surgery's full,' snapped Mrs Allen. 'Come back tomorrow.'

Ben's face grew red. 'It's . . . it's very urgent,' he stuttered. 'I've got some . . . some . . .' Ben found himself quite unable to bring out the word *body*, and his knees began to wobble in a most peculiar way. 'I've got a person. Outside. In the street,' he finished lamely.

'Well, whoever it is will just have to wait their turn like everybody else,' said Mrs Allen. She pushed a numbered plastic disc into Ben's hand and slid the window shut with a bang.

Ben made his way slowly outside, groaning to himself when he glanced down and saw the number on the plastic disc. Number thirteen. It couldn't have been anything else, Ben thought. This was the unluckiest day of his whole life. But worse was still to come.

Ben stepped out into the street. Then his hand came out and clutched at the wall and his mouth opened and shut in helpless astonishment.

The pavement outside the surgery was empty.

There was no Danny. There was no Polly. There was no cart. There was no carpet. *And there was no Granny Price.*

They had all vanished into thin air.

Chapter Five

BEN GAZED FRANTICALLY up and down the street, his heart thumping under his woollen vest. Then he almost cried out in relief as he saw a forlorn little figure coming slowly towards him.

'Polly,' he breathed, kneeling down and putting his arms round her. 'What

happened? Where's Danny? And where's the cart?'

Polly's face was dirty and streaked with tears. She sniffed and hiccupped all the time as she told Ben what had happened.

'Them boys,' she scowled, blowing her nose on Ben's hanky. 'Them nasty boys. They went and stealed your nice cart.'

'Boys?' said Ben, feeling his eyes bulge like gobstoppers. 'What do you mean, Polly? What boys?'

'That Ginger,' sniffed Polly. 'Ginger Wilson. And all that gang. They pushed Danny and he fell down. But I kicked that Ginger on the shin,' she added gleefully, grinning through her tears. Ben gave a silent prayer of thanks that she was safe.

'Good for you, Poll,' he said. 'Come

on, pet. I better take you home now. It's far too late for you to be out.'

Polly put her hand in Ben's and trotted happily beside him.

'Where's Danny now?' said Ben.

'Danny went after them bad boys,' she said. 'He's gonna punch Ginger Wilson on the nose. He's gonna get your cart back for you. *And* Doctor Brown's carpet.'

Ben almost dragged Polly up the lane and bundled her thankfully through the back door of the cottage. Then he ran off in search of his friend.

He didn't have to look far. Ben had only reached the bottom of the lane when he heard wheels squeaking just round the corner. It was Danny Brannigan, limping wearily along, towing Ben's cart behind him. Danny's face was scratched and dirty, his clothes were covered in mud, and he had a large tear in the sleeve of his anorak.

'I got your cart back, Ben,' he announced proudly. Ben peered at Danny in the gloom.

'It must have been some fight,' he said admiringly. 'You don't half look a mess.'

'You should see the others,' grinned Danny, and his teeth gleamed in his dirty face.

Ben had been so glad to see his friend that at first he hadn't even looked at the cart. But now he gave a sudden gasp of horror and his eyes went as round as bicycle wheels. The cart was empty.

'Flippin' heck,' he said, with a very

nasty feeling in his stomach. 'Where's Granny Price?'

Danny hung his head and looked glum. 'I was too late to stop them,' he said dismally. 'They've sold her.'

Ben's legs felt as if the bones had been removed and replaced with spaghetti. His voice didn't seem to be working properly, either.

'Sold her?' he croaked. 'Come off it, Danny.'

'Ginger sold the carpet for fifty pence,' said Danny, with a nervous giggle. 'To old Sol Hamburger, the scrap man. They didn't know what was in it.'

Ben shoved his hands deeper into his pockets and stamped his cold feet on the ground.

'Come on, Danny,' he said, in as firm a voice as he could manage. 'We better get round there before the old man unrolls that carpet and ends up having a heart attack.' And the two boys towed the cart back down the lane towards the junk yard.

Chapter Six

BEN'S BREATH CAME out in clouds of steam as he stood outside the old barn where Solomon Hamburger had his home and his business. He began to bang loudly on the big wooden doors, shouting urgently at the same time.

'Mr Hamburger? Let me in, Mr Hamburger. It's me, Ben Gibson.' The two boys heaved sighs of relief and grinned faintly at one another as they heard feet shuffling towards the door.

'What is it? It's past five o'clock and I'm not open for business,' said a voice

testily, and there stood old Solomon Hamburger. He had wispy white hair down to his shoulders, and a brown wrinkled face like a walnut. He wore an old army greatcoat, tied round the middle with string, and a battered pair of tennis shoes on his feet.

Ben pushed quickly past the scrap dealer into the barn, and his eyes roamed anxiously around the cosy interior. A log fire burned in the fireplace, and piles of the most

fascinating junk lined the walls from floor to ceiling on all sides. Ben often came here to bargain for useful bits of scrap, and this was where he had found the steering wheel for the cart.

'We've come to buy a carpet, Mr Hamburger,' said Ben, grabbing Danny's arm and pointing to where a rolled-up sausage shape lay in a corner. 'That one over there.'

'It's not for sale,' said the old man, shaking his head. 'I've only just bought it. I was going to have a look at it after tea.' He looked at the anxious faces of

the two boys and his eyes narrowed craftily. 'How much will you give me for it?' he said.

Ben rummaged in his pockets. 'How much you got, Danny?' he said.

'Not a bean,' said Danny, showing empty linings. 'Spent the last on them cheese and onion crisps.'

Ben's shoulders slumped as he counted out every penny of the money he'd saved for paint for the cart.

'Two pounds twenty-seven pence?' he offered hopefully, feeling weak with relief when Solomon Hamburger nodded his head.

'Done,' said the old man with satisfaction.

Without wasting any more time Ben pushed open the barn door and wheeled in the cart. He rolled it over the floor to the carpet in the corner.

'Come on, Danny,' he said to his friend. 'This won't take long now.'

'I'll give you a hand,' said the scrap dealer, jingling coins gleefully in his pocket. He tightened the bit of string round his waist and bent down at one end of the carpet. The boys got ready to take the weight at the other end.

'One, two, three, lift,' wheezed the old man.

And then it happened. The most terrifying thing of all. The carpet suddenly began to wriggle and twitch in their grasp, and it gave a ghastly groan that made Dan's scalp prickle with horror.

All three dropped the rolled-up carpet with a thump. Mr Hamburger stood as if turned to stone, like a strange sort of garden gnome. Ben and Danny leaped over a large sofa and peered over the top with round eyes.

The carpet jerked and wriggled some more. Then an angry muffled voice could be heard complaining.

'Where am I? Let me out of here. Help!'

Mr Hamburger said something that made even Ben blush to hear. Then he knelt down on the floor and quickly began to unroll the carpet. And he almost fell over in astonishment when he uncovered the furious red face of Granny Price.

Ben looked at Danny, and Danny looked at Ben, and huge grins spread over both their faces. Granny Price was very much alive.

She sat up, straightened her dress, and pushed back the untidy grey hair that tumbled around her face. She scowled fiercely and pointed a shaking finger at Solomon Hamburger.

'You kidnapped me, you old devil, you,' she shrieked, clenching her fist and waving it furiously in his face.

The old man's mouth opened and closed like a goldfish. Ben and Danny began to roll about on the floor behind the sofa in a helpless fit of laughter. And it took them a very long time to calm down enough to tell their part of the story. The sensible Mr Hamburger helped Granny Price into a chair and put the kettle on, while Ben, still wiping tears from his eyes, began to explain what had happened.

'I reckon it was them mushrooms,' sighed the old lady, when Ben told how they had found her as still as death in her rocking chair. 'They can put you in a coma for hours, sometimes. It's happened before.'

'Well, I'm keeping an eye on you from now on, Becky Price,' declared Solomon Hamburger gruffly, handing her a mug of tea. 'I'll see you never eat

rubbish like that again. It's turned out all right this time, thanks to these brave lads here. But next time you might not wake up at all.'

The two boys left the old couple chatting and squabbling happily over their tea and set off for home at last. Ben had his money safely back in his pocket, for even Solomon Hamburger hadn't the heart to keep it after he'd heard Ben's story.

Ben and Danny parted at the bottom of Blackberry Lane, and Ben grinned at his friend.

'At least we didn't have to take the old witch home,' he said. 'Mr Hamburger can have that pleasure.'

'He won't mind,' said Danny with a snort. 'I reckon he fancies her.'

Ben hooted with laughter. 'You may be right,' he said. Then, towing the cart along behind, he began to trudge up the lane towards home and his waiting tea.